Molly's Monsters

To Jaxon

Hope you enjoy the book

Dan :)

Daniel Hockham

Dedication

For Molly and Isabella

Acknowledgments

Thank you to Gill for bringing Molly's Monsters to life and print at long last!

About the Author

Daniel Hockham is a father of two based in Hampshire. Molly's Monsters was based on his experience when his two daughters were small. It is his first book.

Every morning was the same.

Molly woke up. Her hair was a mess, her bed was a mess, her room was a mess.

"It wasn't like that last night." Dad said, "What have you been doing?"

"It was the monsters." said Molly sleepily.

"Why are you so tired?" asked Mum.

"They keep me up." yawned Molly.

Molly told Mum and Dad all about the monsters; the Tangalies who mess up her hair.

The Covanika who always takes her duvet.

The Hiders who always hide her shoes, slippers and Dad's keys and not forgetting Mr Nobody.

"He's just naughty! He knocks plant pots over, moves things and eats all the biscuits!" Molly exclaimed.

That night as Mum told Molly a bedtime story, she told Molly all about the special monster spray she had made. "It's here on the side if you need it," she said.

As everyone knows monsters are naughty but did you know it's because they don't get enough sleep?

Mum and Dad said, "Goodnight."

No sooner had the door shut the Covanika started pulling at her covers, the light went back on and the Tangalies started to mess up Molly's hair.

The door opened again. It was Dad. "Why have you put the light on?" he asked.

"It was Mr Nobody" said Molly.

"Go to sleep." Dad said, switched off the light again and shut the door.

"Why didn't Dad see all of you?" asked Molly.

"Grownups can't see us!" they laughed.

Molly got up to get the monster spray. What a surprise, one of her slippers was gone and the Tangalies were making a right mess of her hair.

"That's it!" said Molly. "I've had ENOUGH!"

She got the spray from the side and sprayed one big spray towards Mr Nobody who was busy emptying her drawers. He breathed in the sweet smelling spray and took the biggest yawn ever.

The Hiders who were busy unpairing socks also got sprayed. They stopped, gave a big yawn and lay down.

The Covanika was next, by now all of the duvet was on the floor, including the pillow and it was starting on the sheet.

"Big one for you!" said Molly.

He was asleep before he hit the floor.

Molly started putting her bed back together, her clothes away and paired her socks although she still couldn't find her slipper.

She sprayed in all the dark places where monsters seem to live and gave two sprays under the bed...just in case.

Now for you.

She got into the bed, got comfy and gave herself a spray. The Tangalies stopped tying knots in her hair and fell asleep.

Molly let out a big yawn too and fell asleep.

You see, this spray works on all little monsters!

Printed in Great Britain
by Amazon

80451027R00016